The Great TV Turn-Off

Beverly Lewis

Beverly Lewis Books for Young Readers

PICTURE BOOKS

Annika's Secret Wish • *In Jesse's Shoes*
Just Like Mama • *What Is God Like?*
What Is Heaven Like?

THE CUL-DE-SAC KIDS

The Double Dabble Surprise
The Chicken Pox Panic
The Crazy Christmas Angel Mystery
No Grown-ups Allowed
Frog Power
The Mystery of Case D. Luc
The Stinky Sneakers Mystery
Pickle Pizza
Mailbox Mania
The Mudhole Mystery
Fiddlesticks
The Crabby Cat Caper
Tarantula Toes
Green Gravy
Backyard Bandit Mystery
Tree House Trouble
The Creepy Sleep-Over
The Great TV Turn-Off
Piggy Party
The Granny Game
Mystery Mutt
Big Bad Beans
The Upside-Down Day
The Midnight Mystery

Katie and Jake and the Haircut Mistake

www.BeverlyLewis.com

THE CUL-DE-SAC KIDS

The Great TV Turn-Off

—————•—————

Beverly Lewis

BETHANY HOUSE PUBLISHERS
MINNEAPOLIS, MINNESOTA 55438

The Great TV Turn-Off
Copyright © 1998
Beverly Lewis

Cover illustration by Paul Turnbaugh
Text illustrations by Janet Huntington

Published by Bethany House Publishers
11400 Hampshire Avenue South
Bloomington, Minnesota 55438

Bethany House Publishers is a division of
Baker Publishing Group, Grand Rapids, Michigan.

Printed in the United States of America

ISBN 978-1-55661-989-2

Library of Congress Cataloging-in-Publication Data

Lewis, Beverly.
    The great TV turn-off / by Beverly Lewis.
        p. cm. — (The cul-de-sac kids ; 18)
    Summary: Eric and his neighbors on Blossom Hill Lane agree to give up television for one week.
    ISBN 1-55661-989-8 (pbk.)
    [1. Television—Fiction. 2. Neighbors—Fiction. 3. Christian life—Fiction.] I. Title. II. Series: Lewis, Beverly. Cul-de-sac kids ; 18
PZ7.L58464Gp   1997
[Fic]dc21   97–33924
                                             CIP
                                             AC

For
Amanda Hoffman,
who pulled the plug
and lived to tell about it!
And . . .
for her brother,
Jeremy,
also a BIG fan
in the Sunflower State.
(We miss you in Colorado!)

THE CUL-DE-SAC KIDS

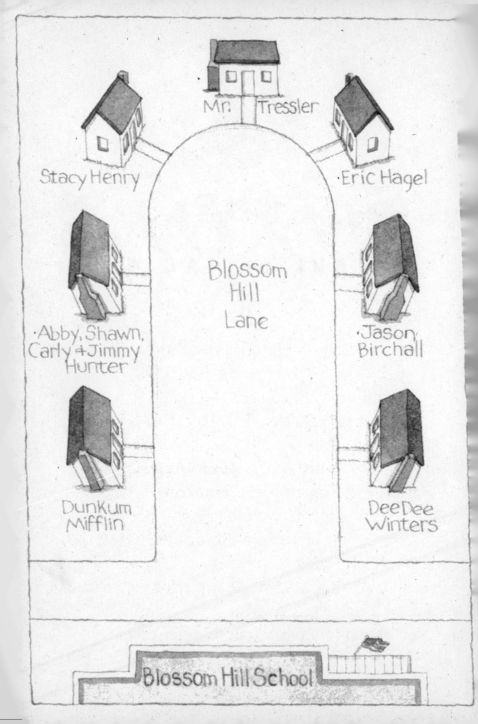

ONE

Eric Hagel slapped the Sunday paper shut. "No TV for me for one whole week. I'm going cold turkey!" he said.

His mother's eyes fluttered. "*What* did you say?"

"You heard right, Mom. America's TV Turn-Off Week starts tomorrow."

Eric's mom cleared off the breakfast table. "Really? My goodness, what a wonderful idea."

"I can't wait to tell my friends," Eric said.

His mother smiled. "Seven days is a

9

long time. Do you think the Cul-de-sac
Kids will go for it?"

"Well, I'm gonna find out," he said.

★ ★ ★

An emergency meeting was held at
Dunkum Mifflin's house. Right after
church.

Abby Hunter sat in the president's
chair—a giant beanbag. "The meeting
will come to order," she said. "Any old
business?"

Eric shook his head. So did Dunkum
and Jason. And so did Stacy, Carly, Dee
Dee, and Abby's Korean brothers—Shawn
and Jimmy Hunter. Nine members,
counting Eric.

"OK, what about new business?"
asked Abby.

Eric spoke up. "Did everyone read the
morning paper? The part about America
turning off the TV?"

The kids just stared at him.

10

"C'mon! Don't you guys read the paper?" he asked.

Abby smiled. "I saw the article."

"So . . . are you with me?" said Eric. "Do you wanna pull the plug?"

"On the tube?" said Jason. "Are you kidding?"

"I think it's a great idea," said Eric. "Just think of all the books you could read."

The others looked shocked.

"Maybe we should have a vote," suggested Abby.

"OK with me," said Eric.

"All in favor of no TV, raise your hands," Abby said.

Eric, Abby, and Dunkum shot their hands up. Then, very slowly, Stacy, Jimmy, and Shawn put theirs up. They were looking around, though, as they voted.

"Last chance to vote," Eric piped up. He was saying it for Dee Dee's and Carly's

11

sake. They were slow-poke members.

"OK," whispered Carly. But she wasn't smiling about it.

"All against no TV, raise your hands," Abby said.

"Wait!" Jason's hand went up, very slowly. "I must be crazy," he muttered.

Abby made the report. "The vote is carried. We pull the plug. *All* of us will."

Jason groaned.

"Hey, you voted for it," Dunkum scolded. "You can't complain now!"

Eric spoke up. "Let's do something totally cool for TV Turn-Off Week."

Jason Birchall's eyes went crossed. "We're skipping TV for a week. Isn't that cool enough?"

"But wait. I have *another* idea," said Eric.

"Let's hear it," said Abby.

The kids listened.

"I think our parents should turn off

the TV, too," Eric said. "No TV for any-one."

Dunkum was nodding his head. "It's only fair," he said.

"What a double dabble good idea!" Abby said, smiling.

Carly raised her hand. She was Abby's sister. "What about Mr. Tressler? He's not anyone's parent. Should he do it?"

Jason couldn't sit still. He was up dancing and jiving. "Good thinking, Carly. But Mr. Tressler lives alone. He watches tons of TV, especially at night. Who's gonna get *him* to agree?"

"Maybe older folks shouldn't be in on it," Abby suggested.

Eric thought about that. "We oughta have the whole cul-de-sac. If everyone in America is doing it, why not Blossom Hill Lane?" he said.

"OK with me," Abby said.

"Then who's gonna break it to Mr. Tressler?" Jason asked.

"I will," Eric spoke up.

"Way to go, Eric!" said Dee Dee.

"I'll go along," Abby offered.

Shawn said in broken English, "I go, too."

So it was set. Eric, Abby, and Shawn would pay a visit to Mr. Tressler.

"Now, what about our parents?" Eric said. "Can we get *them* to black out the tube?"

"We can try!" Dunkum said.

"What if they won't?" Dee Dee asked. "What then?"

The kids were silent. Their brains were buzzing. Especially Eric's. "I've got it!" he said. "If we catch someone sneaking TV time, we pack up the tube. No questions asked."

"Even grown-ups?" asked little Jimmy. His big brown eyes looked bigger than ever.

"Especially grown-ups," Eric said.

"Everyone should sign a promise

15

sheet," Dunkum said.

"I'll make up a bunch," Abby offered.

"And I'll help," Stacy said.

Eric grinned. What a terrific plan!

TWO

Eric knocked on the guest room door. His grandpa's bedroom.

"Come in," Grandpa called.

Eric hoped this wouldn't take long. He hoped his grandpa would agree right away.

"Sit down, sit down," Grandpa said. He was propped up in bed.

Eric pulled up a chair. "Is your afternoon nap over?" he asked.

"*Now* it is." Grandpa smiled a sleepy smile.

"Good, 'cause I have a great idea," Eric

17

said. He began to tell about the TV Turn-Off Week. "We want the grown-ups on the block to join in."

Grandpa rubbed his chin. "Well, well, that *is* an interesting idea."

Eric waited, holding his breath. What would Grandpa say?

"Where'd you come up with this, young man?" asked Grandpa Hagel.

"It was in the morning paper," Eric said. He felt nervous. Should he tell him about the club meeting?

"The newspaper, eh?" Grandpa said.

"I can show it to you," Eric said.

Grandpa waved his hand. "No, no. Don't bother. I've heard of such things. Don't they do this every year?"

Eric said, "Sure do."

"Well, OK. Count me in," said Grandpa.

Yes! Eric was thrilled. "All right!" he hollered.

"Settle down," Grandpa said. "It's not a big deal."

"It *is* a big deal," Eric said. "Thanks, Grandpa!"

Eric went over to the big bed. "Any ideas about Mom? How can I get *her* to give up TV?" he asked.

Grandpa scratched his head. "Well now, that's gonna be tricky. She loves her exercise shows."

Eric wondered what to do. "Do you think she'll sign the promise sheet?"

"Never hurts to ask," said Grandpa.

"True," said Eric. But he knew his mom might not sign.

In fact, there was a strong chance she'd say no.

★ ★ ★

Bri-i-i-ing!
Eric hurried to answer the phone.
"Sign-up sheets are ready," Abby said.
"Good! I'll be right over," Eric replied.

19

"How'd it go with your grandpa?" asked Abby.

"Easy as pie," said Eric. "Now, if I can just get my mom to listen."

"How hard can it be?" Abby said. "She'll wanna go along with all the neighbors. Won't she?"

"She'll wanna keep up with her exercises, too," Eric told her.

"Oh, I forgot. She's into fitness," said Abby.

"Well, wish me luck," said Eric.

"I'll *pray* for you," Abby said.

Eric knew she would.

"When should we visit Mr. Tressler?" Abby asked.

"Before supper tonight," Eric suggested.

"OK."

"I'll come over soon. After I talk to my mom," Eric said.

"See ya later, alligator," Abby said.

20

"After a while, crocodile," Eric answered.

"Next time, porcupine," Abby added.

"Not too soon, baboon," Eric replied.

"Okey-dokey, artichokey," Abby said.

"Bye-bye, horsefly," Eric finished.

THREE

Eric rang the door at the Hunters' house. Carly and Jimmy came to the door together. They were dressed like Bible characters.

"We're David and Goliath. Wanna see our play?" Carly said.

Eric smiled. "Maybe later. I have to talk to Abby."

Carly rolled her eyes. "Oh, you came to see *Abby*, didn't you?"

"Cut the comedy," he said. "Where's your sister?"

Jimmy grinned up at him. "Better

watch out," he said. He held up his sling-shot. "I come in name of God!"

"That's what David's supposed to tell Goliath," Eric said. "Here, point your slingshot at Carly."

"She not Carly Anne Hunter. Now sister is BIG giant!" Jimmy shouted.

Eric had never heard Jimmy talk so loud. But then, Jimmy hadn't heard Bible stories before. Not till he came to America last Thanksgiving.

"Come in and wait. I'll go get Abby," said Carly, the enemy giant.

Jimmy zipped off after her. Eric saw him hold out his slingshot.

Eric ended up waiting in the kitchen. It was impossible *not* to wander in there. Mrs. Hunter was making chocolate chip cookies. They were still warm. And the chocolate pieces were all gooey when she gave him one.

"M-m-m, thanks!" Eric said. "My favorite."

"Everybody's favorite," Mrs. Hunter agreed.

Soon, Abby and Shawn came downstairs. They had a bunch of papers. "Here they are," Abby said.

Eric looked at the sign-up sheets. And Shawn ate cookies.

The promise sheet was very cool. It said the following:

I promise not to watch TV for one whole week. I will not turn on the TV set from March 2 through March 8. If I am caught sneaking TV, The Cul-de-sac Kids will box up my TV. They'll put it away. On March 8, my TV will be returned.

Signed: _____

"Hey, this is great," Eric said. "How'd you think this up?"

Abby shrugged. "It's nothing much. Anybody could've done it."

"Not *this* body," Eric said and laughed.

24

Abby reached for a cookie. "This is my third one," she whispered. "Here, have another."

Eric thought she'd never ask. "Thanks," he said.

"Want some milk to go with it?" Abby asked.

"Sure!"

Abby poured milk for Eric. Then for her brother Shawn.

They drank milk and ate warm cookies together. They watched the David and Goliath show. But the story ended too quickly. Goliath (Carly) turned the slingshot on David (little Jimmy.)

"That's not how the story goes," Abby said, giggling.

Eric hooted with laughter.

Then Mrs. Hunter tempted the future king of Israel. She did it by bringing out more cookies.

Wicked Goliath spied them. She declared, "Time out. The play is over."

"Not over!" Little David whined and fussed. He took a handful of cookies. "Time for chocolate manna!"

"That's a *different* story," Eric said.

"Eric's right," said Mrs. Hunter. "You may continue the play tomorrow."

"Yay! We'll do a play instead of watching TV," Abby said. Then she showed her mother the sign-up sheet.

"What's this?" Mrs. Hunter said.

"Take a look," Abby said.

Eric wondered what would happen. He crossed his fingers behind his back. Would Mrs. Hunter promise no TV? Would she sign?

"We want the whole cul-de-sac to agree," Abby said softly. "One hundred percent."

Jimmy wiped his mouth. "Jimmy sign now!"

"Wait a minute," Mrs. Hunter said. She found a pen in her kitchen drawer. "Ladies first." She was smiling.

The kids watched Mrs. Hunter sign her name.

"Cool! You're the first on the block," Eric said.

Mrs. Hunter twirled around the kitchen. The kids clapped and cheered. Especially Eric.

After all, it was *his* idea.

Now . . . off to Mr. Tressler's house!

Would the old gentleman want to be cool, too?

FOUR

Eric, Abby, and Shawn crossed the street. They headed for Mr. Tressler's house at the end of the cul-de-sac.

"Hide the sign-up sheet," Eric said.

"How come?" asked Abby.

"Mr. Tressler not like?" Shawn asked.

"We should just go for a visit. After we're there awhile, we'll tell him about the TV turn-off," Eric suggested.

"Double dabble good idea," Abby said. She folded the paper and put it in her jacket.

Shawn nodded. "Eric is right."

So they just visited. They talked about Mr. Tressler's doves. But their neighbor wanted to talk about TV.

"Have you watched the Adventure Channel?" he asked.

"Sometimes," Eric said.

"We don't watch TV during supper," Abby said.

"Not good for family talking," Shawn said.

"Well, I'd pay double for it," Mr. Tressler said.

Gulp! Eric was worried.

"Did any of you see the dolphin show?" Mr. Tressler asked.

"When?" Eric asked.

Mr. Tressler glanced at the ceiling. He was thinking. "Two nights ago, I believe."

"I see dolphins in books," Shawn spoke up. "I see them swim with people."

Mr. Tressler's face lit up. "That's it! That's like the show I saw." He seemed so pleased. Really delighted. He kept talking

30

about the one-hour show.

Eric tried to catch Abby's eye. He made several motions with his hands.

Finally, she looked at him.

Eric pointed to the pocket in her jacket.

Then Abby caught on. She pulled out one of the sign-up sheets.

Eric nodded. *Good!* Now maybe they could discuss their plan. He was about to bring up the subject. But he stopped.

Mr. Tressler was reaching for the TV remote control.

What's he doing? Eric wondered.

"Say, would you like to watch TV with me?" Mr. Tressler glanced at the wall clock. "One of my favorite shows is coming on. How about it?"

Poor Mr. Tressler. He was looking around at each of them. Shawn, Abby, and Eric were silent. They didn't know what to do or say.

At last, Eric spoke up. "OK, we'll watch your show."

Abby's eyes blinked with surprise.

"We'll watch with you. But it could be the *last* one you see. Till next week, that is," Eric said.

"Excuse me?" Mr. Tressler pulled on his bow tie.

Eric crossed the room. He took a sign-up sheet from Abby. "Let me explain."

Mr. Tressler was frowning. "Please do," he said.

"America is turning off the tube," Eric said. "Starting tomorrow, no TV."

"We want the whole block to join in," Abby said.

Shawn was nodding. "Cul-de-sac Kids and grown-ups no watch television. One whole week," he said.

Mr. Tressler gasped a bit. "How will I enjoy my meals? I *always* watch the news during supper."

"What about the radio?" Abby asked.

"You could *listen* to the news."

"Great idea!" Eric said.

Mr. Tressler shook his head. "It's not the same."

"Maybe better," Shawn said. "Use more imagination."

Mr. Tressler began to chuckle. "You kids want this badly. I can see that."

Eric nodded his head. "We sure do!"

"Well, I don't know. . . ." The old man paused. "It's awfully lonely in this house."

Eric felt sorry for his neighbor. "Why don't you have supper with us? My grandpa will miss TV, too. You'd be good company for each other," he said.

Abby and Shawn were grinning.

Mr. Tressler sighed. "The world might stop spinning without TV," he said. "Why don't you go ahead? Leave this old man out of it."

"No, no, Mr. Tressler. We *want* you in on the fun," Abby insisted.

Fun? Who said it would be fun? Eric

scratched his head. Maybe Mr. Tressler was right. Maybe only certain people should do the turn-off thing.

Going without TV might be boring. What would *he* do all week without it?

Seven days was a very long time.

FIVE

Eric could hardly watch Mr. Tressler's show. The dolphins were fine. It wasn't that. He just kept thinking about next week.

No TV? Was he crazy?

Maybe it was time for another club meeting. An emergency meeting, for sure.

But wait. The Cul-de-sac Kids might call him a wimp.

He could almost hear little Dee Dee Winters. She'd be giggling herself silly. "You gotta be tough, Eric," she might say.

"Can't you read books or play ball or something else?"

He wouldn't be wimpy. He'd made the choice. Everyone else was jumping on board. Except Mr. Tressler. And maybe Eric's own mother.

He looked at his watch. There was a commercial on TV. "I need to talk to my mom," he spoke up.

Mr. Tressler perked up his ears. "Is your mother giving up TV?"

"I haven't asked her yet," Eric answered.

Shawn got up and stretched. "I ready," he said.

"Don't you want to watch the rest?" Mr. Tressler asked.

Abby stood up. "We do, and we don't." She held up the promise sheet. "It's almost dark. We wanna talk to some more neighbors."

Mr. Tressler seemed a bit sad. "Don't go away mad," he said.

"Oh, we're not," said Abby. "It's your choice."

"Free country," Shawn piped up.

"You're right about that," Mr. Tressler said. "But thanks for asking anyway."

"Any time," Eric muttered.

Rats!

How many more people wouldn't sign?

★ ★ ★

Eric took two promise sheets into the house. He found his mother in the kitchen. She was warming up leftovers. They always had leftovers for Sunday supper.

"Hey, Mom," he said.

She glanced at him. "What's that?"

He put the sign-up sheet on the counter. "Just something. It's kinda dumb, I guess."

Grandpa came into the room just then. "Why so gloomy?" he asked Eric.

37

"Things aren't working out," Eric muttered.

"What things?" his mother asked.

Eric told her everything. Mostly about Mr. Tressler's TV habit. "He says he can't eat supper without the news."

"That's funny," Grandpa spoke up. "The evening news gives *me* a stomach pain!"

Eric had to laugh. "Good one, Grandpa. I'll have to try *that* on Mr. Tressler."

"Be my guest," said Grandpa. "The old fella needs a boot in the pants."

"Now, Grandpa!" Eric's mother scolded.

"Excuse me, but it's true. Let's see what I can do?" Grandpa said. "First off, *I* want to sign up for turn-off torture."

Eric laughed out loud.

Grandpa gazed at Eric's mother. "And what about the fair, young maiden?"

Eric's mother shook her head. "I can't

go without exercising. I really can't."

"You could run up and down the cul-de-sac," Eric suggested. "No one'll mind. Right, Grandpa?"

Grandpa nodded cheerfully. "Eric's absolutely right."

"Are *all* the neighbors signing?" Eric's mother asked.

"The kids are asking their parents right now." After all, they didn't have much longer. Tomorrow was the first day.

"Well, OK. I won't be a party pooper." Eric's mother signed her name. "I hope I don't live to regret this." She rubbed her hips.

"You won't," promised Eric. He hoped it was true.

★ ★ ★

Eric had to call Abby. "Everyone at *my* house signed," he bragged.

"So did all the Hunter family," Abby said.

"What about Dunkum and Jason? Any problems?" Eric asked.

"They've already called in to report," Abby said. "And Stacy didn't have trouble, either."

"Maybe 'cause her mom works," Eric reminded Abby.

"But after a long day, some people like to veg out in front of the TV," Abby said. "Stacy's mom is a good sport."

Eric knew she was right. "What about Mr. Tressler?" he asked. "Should we just let it go? Let him spoil our block record?"

"Guess so," Abby said. "It's not for a school grade or anything."

"No kidding." Eric was glad it wasn't a test.

They talked a little more. About their pets—Abby's dog and Eric's hamster.

Then he heard a knock. "Someone's at the door."

"See ya at school tomorrow," Abby said. "Remember, no TV."

"How can I forget?" he teased.

They hung up and Eric hurried to the door.

There stood Mr. Tressler.

"Well, hello," Eric said. "What are *you* doing here?"

"Let's talk," said the old gentleman.

"Cool," said Eric.

SIX

"Come in," said Eric. He took his neighbor's coat and hat.

"Thank you," Mr. Tressler said.

Eric led him to the living room. "Have a seat."

Mr. Tressler chose Grandpa's chair. "I've been thinking," he said.

"Yes?"

"Am I the only coward in the cul-de-sac?" asked Mr. T.

"Coward?" said Eric. "What do you mean?"

The old man stared at his cane. "What

I mean is, I want to sign on the dotted line."

"You do?" Eric nearly shouted.

"Where's that promise sheet or whatever?" Mr. Tressler said.

Eric stood up. He glanced out the window. "Don't go away. I'll be right back!"

He dashed out the front door. Even forgot to put on his coat. He headed across the street to Abby's.

Soon, he was back. "Here's the sign-up sheet. Read it carefully," Eric warned.

Mr. Tressler frowned. "Why's that?"

"Abby's pretty smart. She wrote all this stuff." He pointed out the part about boxing up the TV. "But you shouldn't worry. That won't happen to you."

"Never fear. I'll suffer through," said Mr. T.

Eric grinned. "I'm glad you came over. And don't forget, you can have supper with us."

"Better talk to your mother," Mr. T said.

"She'll call you, OK?"

"Wonderful." The old man seemed mighty thrilled.

"Table talk at our house is better than the news anytime." Eric got Mr. Tressler's coat and hat.

"Tell your grandad hello for me," said Mr. T.

"Sure will," said Eric. "He's probably upstairs watching TV. Getting his last fix, you know?"

Mr. T waved his cane and gave a wink.

Eric watched the old man walk down the sidewalk.

Ya-hoo!

One hundred percent for Blossom Hill Lane!

He ran upstairs and watched TV with Grandpa. Last chance.

SEVEN

"It's Monday, the first day of TV Turn-Off Week," Eric's teacher told the class. "I pulled the plug on my TV. How many of you did, too?"

Eric was proud to raise his hand. He looked around the room. All the kids had their hands up.

"That's really terrific," said Miss Hershey.

Eric wanted to check out lots of books from the school library. Abby, Stacy, and Dunkum were going to meet him there. Shawn and Jason had other plans. They were going to ice skate till their legs hurt.

Going without TV wouldn't be easy. Anybody knew that.

And it *wasn't* easy.

It was horrible.

★ ★ ★

After school, Eric kept staring at the black TV. It was turned off, of course. But he looked at it anyway. Even his stack of books didn't help.

"What a nightmare," he muttered.

Eric went upstairs. On the way, he passed the guest room—Grandpa's. The small TV seemed to stare at *him*. He turned his head away.

"That you, Eric?" Grandpa called.

Eric peeked into the room. He held his head funny. That was so he couldn't see the dark TV. "Hi, Grandpa," he said.

Grandpa tilted his head, too. "Something the matter?" He chuckled.

"Oh, nothing," Eric said. But his eyes

47

were drawn to the silent tube. The one-eyed monster!

Suddenly, Grandpa reached for the TV remote.

"No! Don't do that!" Eric shouted.

Grandpa dropped the remote on his bed. "Gotcha!"

"Aw, don't scare me," pleaded Eric. "I thought you forgot already."

Grandpa shook his head. "I made a promise. I'll keep it."

Eric eyed the remote. "Maybe you'd better put that away."

"Good thinking," he said. "Here."

Eric put the remote high in the closet. "Don't forget where it is," he said.

Grandpa reached for a bag of jelly beans. "Any ideas?"

"For what?"

"For keeping my brain busy," said Grandpa.

"I've got a bunch of books," Eric told him.

Grandpa was grinning. "Good choice. Let's read one together. Maybe we can discuss it later."

It sounded OK to Eric. Almost like school, though. "What's your favorite?" he asked.

"Got a good mystery?" Grandpa asked.

"I'll check." Eric went back downstairs. He found an adventure mystery. "We need some popcorn, too," he said to himself.

His mother was chopping cabbage in the kitchen. "Hi, Eric. How's cold turkey going?"

He shook his head. "So far, it's horrible. I think Grandpa's fading fast," he said. "What about you? Did you do your exercises?"

She nodded. "I ran around the cul-de-sac six times."

"Really?"

"The neighbors must think I'm nuts," she said.

49

"How come?" asked Eric.

"Well, Mr. Tressler came outside. He asked if I was all right." She laughed.

"What did you tell him?" Eric asked.

"I said I was in withdrawal," she replied.

Eric understood. "Then what?"

"Mr. Tressler stayed outside, too. He walked around his driveway," she said. "And every time I came around the corner, he'd wave."

"It's about time Mr. T got some fresh air." Eric was glad. The Great TV Turn-Off was doing *somebody* some good.

"I invited him for supper tomorrow night," his mother said.

"That'll be cool," said Eric. "I like Mr. Tressler." He almost forgot why he'd come to the kitchen.

Then his mother said, "Want some popcorn?"

"How'd you know?" he said.

"You have that look," she said.

Eric grinned. "Thanks, Mom."

Just then they heard thumps overhead.

"Sounds like Grandpa dropped a shoe," Eric said.

"Probably on purpose," his mother said. "Better get back upstairs. I'll bring the popcorn."

Eric closed his eyes as he passed the living room. He felt his way to the stairs.

Why did the TV keep pulling him, anyway?

EIGHT

Tuesday was the second day of TV Turn-Off.

Pure misery.

All of Eric's favorite after-school specials were on. But he wouldn't watch them. He'd promised.

Everyone else was stuck, too. "All across America," he reminded himself. "Everybody's bored. Just like me."

Grandpa came downstairs for tea. First time in a long time. "Where's that mystery book of yours?" he asked.

Eric found it. "Here you go," he said.

Grandpa settled into his favorite chair. "Now, where were we?" And he began to read.

Eric enjoyed hearing Grandpa. Sometimes he would change his voice around. It made the characters almost real.

By suppertime, Grandpa had to stop. "Help your mother set the table," he said.

Eric wanted to know what happened. "Can we read after supper?"

"Only if you read to *me*," Grandpa said.

"It's a deal!"

★ ★ ★

Mr. Tressler showed up on time for supper. He was dressed up. Nice coat and suspenders. The works.

"Welcome, neighbor," Grandpa said.

Eric held the door open. He was glad to do it. Having their neighbor come for a meal was a great idea. It might keep Mr. T from sneaking TV.

"Whatcha been doing?" Eric asked him.

"I've got a lot of time on my hands," Mr. Tressler answered. "Don't really know what to do with myself."

"I know what you mean," Eric agreed.

Grandpa waved them into the living room. "Let's chat by the fire," he said.

Eric's mother offered some hot tea.

"Thank you, don't mind if I do," said Mr. T.

Grandpa struck up a conversation. He and Mr. T talked about their birds. Doves, canaries, and parakeets. They laughed every so often. They all sipped tea.

Eric couldn't remember listening to two old men chatter. It was kinda fun. And for several minutes he forgot. He forgot that he missed TV!

After supper, his mother brought out some games. "Anybody interested in playing Monopoly?" she asked.

Mr. Tressler's eyes lit up. "I used to

play that game as a teenager. It's been a long, long time."

Grandpa was ready to take on Mr. T. He seemed eager to shuffle the cards.

Eric got excited, too. "Are you gonna play?" he asked his mother.

She pulled out a chair. "Count me in!"

They played till Eric's bedtime. The mantel clock struck nine times.

"Wow, I can't believe it!" he said.

Mr. Tressler scooted his chair back. "Time flies when you're having fun."

"You can say that again!" Grandpa answered.

Eric piped up. "Time flies when you're—"

"Enough!" his mother scolded.

"Sorry, Mom," he said.

They were all grinning at him now.

"Thanks for a great evening," Mr. T said.

"Any time," Grandpa said.

"How about my place next time?" Mr. T offered.

Eric's mother smiled. "We'd love to come."

"Can you cook?" Eric asked.

Mr. Tressler laughed out loud. "You'll have to judge that for yourself, young man."

They said their good-byes.

Before Eric went to bed, he hugged his mom. "I didn't miss the TV all night," he whispered.

She kissed his head. "Me neither."

Eric could hardly wait to see the Cul-de-sac Kids. How were his friends doing without the tube?

NINE

Wednesday morning was crazy.

Eric got up early for his paper route. He felt tired. He'd gone to bed late. But playing Monopoly last night was worth it.

He bundled up to go outdoors. It was snowing softly.

First stop, Mr. Tressler's house.

Usually he heard flute music this early. Mr. T liked to practice before sunrise. It was his special thing.

Eric was used to it. The old man wasn't weird. Not really.

Eric tossed the paper onto the porch.

Phhhhlat! It bounced off the railing.

"I can do better than that." He went to find the paper. Then he carried it up onto the porch.

That's when he heard something. It sounded like the voice of a news reporter. He didn't want to snoop. But he was curious.

Eric took a quick peek. Through the door window he saw a flashing light.

"Oh no!" he said. "Mr. T's in trouble now!"

Sure enough. The TV in the living room was on.

He wondered what to do.

Eric took another peek. *This* time he saw Mr. T lying on the sofa. Sound asleep.

★   ★   ★

At school, Eric told his friends what he'd seen.

"Maybe his TV came on by itself," Jason said, laughing.

"TVs don't do that," Eric argued.

Abby nodded. "Eric's right."

"Eric's *always* right," Dee Dee piped up. "I'm sick of it!" She ran to the merry-go-round.

"What's wrong with her?" Eric said.

"She's a little freaked out. We *all* are," Carly said. "Giving up TV is a big deal."

Abby shook her head. "But a promise is a promise."

"Rules are rules," said Dunkum.

Eric agreed. "Mr. T loses his TV."

"First thing after school," Jason said.

"Poor Mr. Tressler," Stacy said. "Do we *really* have to box it up?"

Abby reminded her of the promise sheet. "We all signed it. Remember?"

"What if Mr. T just forgot?" said Dunkum. "What about that?"

Jason squeezed into the circle. "Maybe his TV got lonely."

Nobody paid attention.

"Has anyone *almost* turned on their TV?" Eric asked.

Shawn and Jimmy looked at each other. "I not," said Jimmy. "I see Shawn, though."

Eric perked up his ears. "Surely not Shawn," he said.

Shawn nodded his head. "I come very close." It sounded like *velly*.

Abby twisted her hair. "Maybe we should have lots of club meetings this week," she said. "To keep us out of trouble."

"Good idea," Stacy said. "Let's meet at my house after school."

"First we have to visit Mr. Tressler," Eric said.

"That's true," Abby said. "Who's coming along?"

Nobody blinked an eye.

Eric looked at Abby. "Guess it's you and me."

Abby looked around. "Well, that's settled. Eric and I are stuck with the dirty work."

"Spread the word at morning recess," Eric said. "We'll have a club meeting at Stacy's."

"Jimmy and I could put on a play," Carly suggested.

Abby grinned. "David kills Goliath, right?"

"Or the other way around," Carly said.

The school bell rang.

"Bye!" they all called to one another.

Eric ran to the outside door. He was worried. He felt funny. Promise sheet or not.

Was it right to take away an old man's TV?

TEN

Eric rang Mr. Tressler's doorbell. "Are you nervous?" he asked Abby.

"A little," she said.

"Who should do the talking?" he asked.

"You can," she said.

That's when the door opened.

"Good afternoon, Mr. Tressler," they said.

"Hello there, kids," he said. "Come in."

Eric glanced at the TV. *Good*, he thought. *It's off*.

"What can I do for you?" Mr. Tressler asked.

Eric got straight to the point. "Your TV was turned on this morning."

"Oh?" Mr. Tressler said.

"Yes, I was delivering your newspaper. That's when I heard it," Eric said.

Mr. T frowned. "That's funny. I don't remember."

"You don't?" Eric was puzzled.

"Not at all." The old man pulled on his ear. "That's very strange."

Eric looked at Abby. She shrugged back at him. She didn't seem to know what to say, either.

"I saw something else," Eric spoke up. "You were asleep on your couch."

Mr. Tressler looked surprised. "Oh, that's right. I fell asleep there. But I never turned on the TV."

"How could it turn on itself?" Eric knew it sounded ridiculous. "Could you have bumped the remote?"

"Well, I don't know," replied Mr. T. He got up and walked the length of the room. He seemed to be thinking very hard.

"Are you okay?" Abby asked.

"Fine and dandy," he replied. "Now, just a minute. It's coming back to me."

Eric waited. So did Abby.

"I woke up late last night. Needed some warm milk," Mr. T explained. "I was a little under the weather. So I stayed downstairs on the couch. Must've fallen asleep."

Eric wanted to hear how the TV got turned on.

"Yes, yes. I remember now," said Mr. T. "When I awakened this morning, the TV was going. And I was lying on the couch."

Eric and Abby stared at each other. They still didn't know what to say.

"I turned it off immediately," Mr. Tressler told them.

Eric scratched his head. He got up and stood at the window. He thought everything over. "Do you ever talk in your sleep?" he asked.

"Don't know that I do" came the reply.

"Have you ever walked in your sleep?" Eric asked.

"How would I know?" Mr. T chuckled. "But you know, it's very possible . . ." He paused.

What? Eric wondered. *What's he gonna say?*

Eric waited, dying to know.

Mr. Tressler sighed. "I may have turned on the TV in my sleep. Out of pure habit." He looked at Eric and Abby. "If so, I'm truly sorry."

Eric felt sorry, too. "I guess we could give you a second chance," he said.

Mr. Tressler shook his head. "Oh no! We play by the rules around here. I signed that sheet of yours. So that's that!"

★ ★ ★

Eric felt odd. He didn't want to follow

through with this. Not when Mr. T had been asleep!

"It doesn't seem fair," he said.

Abby held the box. "Mr. Tressler's a good sport," she said.

"I insist," said the old man. Then he motioned them into the kitchen. "There's another little TV out here."

Eric couldn't believe it. Mr. Tressler was gonna make them box up *both* his TVs!

When the boxes were sealed and put away, Mr. Tressler smiled. "It's fun living on this street," he said. "You Cul-de-sac Kids are great."

Abby gave Mr. Tressler a hug. "Only four days to go," she whispered. "Will you be all right?"

"Absolutely," Mr. T replied. "I'll play my flute more. Maybe even at night!"

They laughed with him.

Eric shook his neighbor's hand. "Sorry about all this," he said.

"No need," said Mr. T. "I got what was coming to me."

Eric and Abby said good-bye and walked home. "Guess we oughta think things over next year," Eric said.

"I know what you mean," Abby said. "That was tough."

"Sure was," said Eric.

ELEVEN

Eric met Jason at Eric's front door. "What's up?" Eric asked.

"We have to talk," Jason said.

"What about?" Eric said.

"The Great TV Turn-Off idea," Jason said. "It's . . . it's, uh—"

"If you don't like it, say so," Eric said. He was sure Jason was having a hard time. His friend was probably bored silly.

"Listen, you were right about blacking out the tube," Jason said. "I can't believe how good I feel."

Eric could hardly believe his ears!

"I have gobs more time to do stuff. I've started building Lego projects again," he said. "My parents and I have time to talk to one another."

"Cool," said Eric.

Jason's face looked like Christmas morning. "I'm glad you got us to turn off the TV, Eric," said Jason. "It was the best idea you've ever had."

Eric told him about eating supper with Mr. Tressler. He told about playing games and reading books out loud. "And Mr. Tressler's gonna cook us supper," he said. "Unreal, huh?"

"Wow, that's cool!" replied Jason.

"Very cool," said Eric. "And we're only through the first half of the week. Just think what good friends we're all gonna be!"

Jason pushed up his glasses. He clicked his fingers. "Hey, I've got an idea. Let's turn off the TV forever!"

"Get real," Eric said.

71

"I'm *serious*! So . . . what do you think?" Jason was pushing it.

"Better wait till the end of this week. We should have a club meeting about it," Eric said.

"Cool!" Jason dashed out the door.

"See ya," Eric called.

His mother was doing sit-ups in the kitchen. "How was your day?" she asked.

"Better than ever." He told her about Mr. Tressler's two TVs. "He made us box both of them up."

His mother stopped her exercises. "That's amazing."

"I think I got something started," he explained. "Something Abby might call 'double dabble good.' "

His mother did a thumbs up. "That's my boy."

Eric grinned. He was dying for his mystery book. And to hear his grandpa's many different reading voices.

He walked past the living room. Didn't

even close his eyes this time.

Nope.

The TV didn't stare back at him. Didn't call to him. Didn't even pull at him.

Not one bit!

THE CUL-DE-SAC KIDS SERIES

Don't miss #19!
PIGGY PARTY

Carly Hunter is chosen to take the class pet home for the weekend, in time for Groundhog's Day. Tired of winter, she decides to test the guinea pig's eye for weather-telling.

Can "Piggy" guess the beginning of spring? Will he see his shadow like his famous cousin back east?

When the Cul-de-sac Kids hear of Carly's outdoor experiment, they ask to join in. All the pets on Blossom Hill Lane show up (with their owners, of course!) at the Piggy Party, including Jason's fussy frog and Dee Dee's crabby cat.

About the Author

Beverly Lewis will never forget her own TV Turn-Off Week. It happened one summer in northern Minnesota. The family was spending a week in a cabin near Duluth. "All of us agreed to it," she says. "We talked to each other more. Our kids did many creative things. We even discussed the birds and the bees!"

Beverly offers a challenge for her readers to turn off the tube. "You might decide to unplug it forever," she says. "Remember, Jason Birchall wanted to!"

Do you like action and mystery? Plenty of humor? Then you'll love the entire collection of The Cul-de-sac Kids!

Also by Beverly Lewis

The Beverly Lewis Amish Heritage Cookbook

GIRLS ONLY (GO!)†
Youth Fiction

Girls Only! Volume One
Girls Only! Volume Two

SUMMERHILL SECRETS‡
Youth Fiction

SummerHill Secrets: Volume One
SummerHill Secrets: Volume Two

HOLLY'S HEART
Youth Fiction

Holly's Heart: Collection One‡
Holly's Heart: Collection Two‡
Holly's Heart: Collection Three†

SEASONS OF GRACE
Adult Fiction

The Secret

ABRAM'S DAUGHTERS
Adult Fiction

The Covenant • *The Betrayal* • *The Sacrifice*
The Prodigal • *The Revelation*

ANNIE'S PEOPLE
Adult Fiction

The Preacher's Daughter • *The Englisher* • *The Brethren*

COURTSHIP OF NELLIE FISHER
Adult Fiction

The Parting • *The Forbidden* • *The Longing*

THE HERITAGE OF LANCASTER COUNTY
Adult Fiction

The Shunning • *The Confession* • *The Reckoning*

OTHER ADULT FICTION

The Postcard • *The Crossroad* • *The Redemption of Sarah Cain*
October Song • *Sanctuary** • *The Sunroom*

www.BeverlyLewis.com

*with David Lewis   †4 books in each volume   ‡5 books in each volume

From Bethany House Publishers

Fiction for Young Readers
(ages 7–10)

AstroKids™
by Robert Elmer

Space scooters? Floating robots? Jupiter ice cream? Blast into the future for out-of-this-world, zero-gravity fun with the AstroKids on space station *CLEO-7*.

The Cul-de-sac Kids
by Beverly Lewis

Each story in this lighthearted series features the hilarious antics and predicaments of nine endearing boys and girls who live on Blossom Hill Lane.

Janette Oke's Animal Friends
by Janette Oke

Endearing creatures from the farm, forest, and zoo discover their place in God's world through various struggles, mishaps, and adventures.